n Thomas

Beach Lane Books

New York   London   Toronto   Sydney   New Delhi

For Kathy!

BEACH LANE BOOKS

An imprint of Simon & Schuster Children's Publishing Division

1230 Avenue of the Americas, New York, New York 10020

© 2022 by Jan Thomas

Book design by Rebecca Syracuse © 2022 by Simon & Schuster, Inc.

For information about special discounts for bulk purchases, please contact Simon & Schuster Special Sales at 1-866-506-1949 or business@simonandschuster.com.

The Simon & Schuster Speakers Bureau can bring authors to your live event. For more information or to book an event, contact the Simon & Schuster Speakers Bureau at 1-866-248-3049 or visit our website at www.simonspeakers.com.

The text for this book was set in Chaloops.

The illustrations for this book were rendered digitally.

Manufactured in China

0522 SCP

First Edition

2 4 6 8 10 9 7 5 3 1

Library of Congress Cataloging-in-Publication Data

Names: Thomas, Jan, 1958– author.

Title: Even robots can be thankful! / Jan Thomas.

Description: First edition. | New York : Beach Lane Books, [2022] | Audience: Ages 0-8. | Audience: Grades 2-3. | Summary: In three stories, Red Robot and Blue Robot learn that gratitude is not always easy, but best friends are something to be thankful for.

Identifiers: LCCN 2021060566 (print) | LCCN 2021060567 (ebook) | ISBN 9781665911672 (hardcover) | ISBN 9781665911689 (ebook)

Subjects: CYAC: Best friends—Fiction. | Friendship—Fiction. | Gratitude—Fiction. | Robots—Fiction. | Humorous stories. | LCGFT: Humorous stories.

Classification: LCC PZ7.T36694 Eve 2022 (print) | LCC PZ7.T36694 (ebook) | DDC [E]—dc23

LC record available at https://lccn.loc.gov/2021060566

LC ebook record available at https://lccn.loc.gov/2021060567

CONTENTS

BUMP IN THE NIGHT

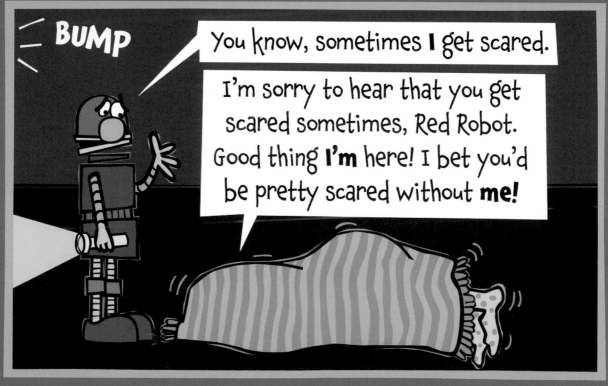

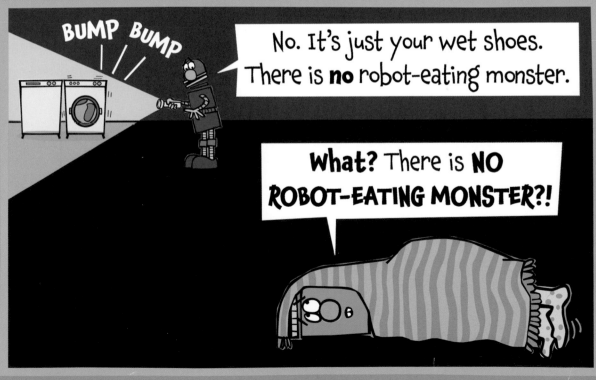

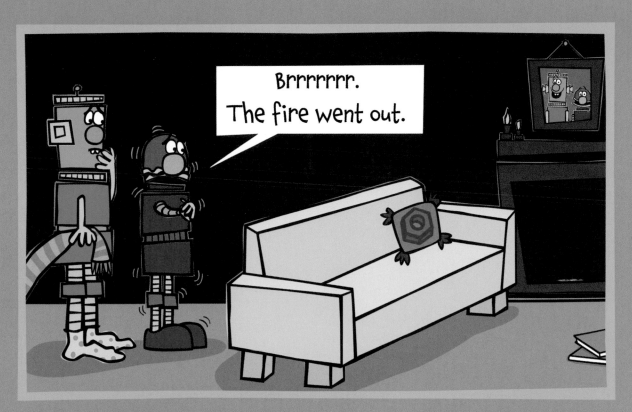

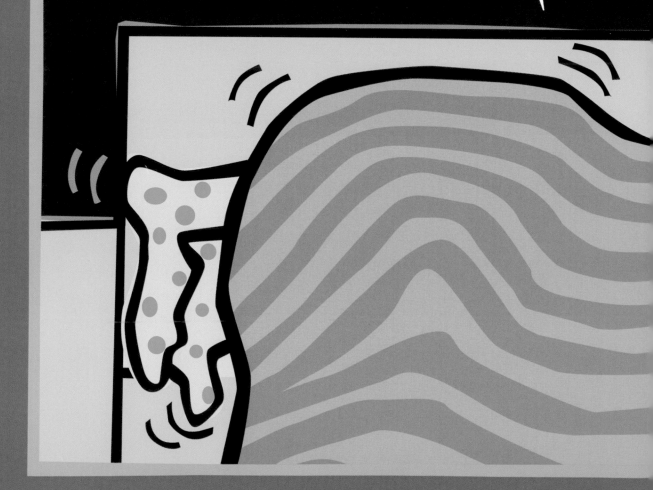

SORTING BOLTS

THE TRAIN TRIP

Oh! It looks like Red Robot has an envelope with a **train ticket** inside!

I wonder **why** Red Robot has an envelope with a **train ticket** inside?

Maybe it's because Red Robot is going on a **TRAIN TRIP!**

Oh dear. **What** would it be like if Red Robot **went away on a TRAIN TRIP . . . ?**

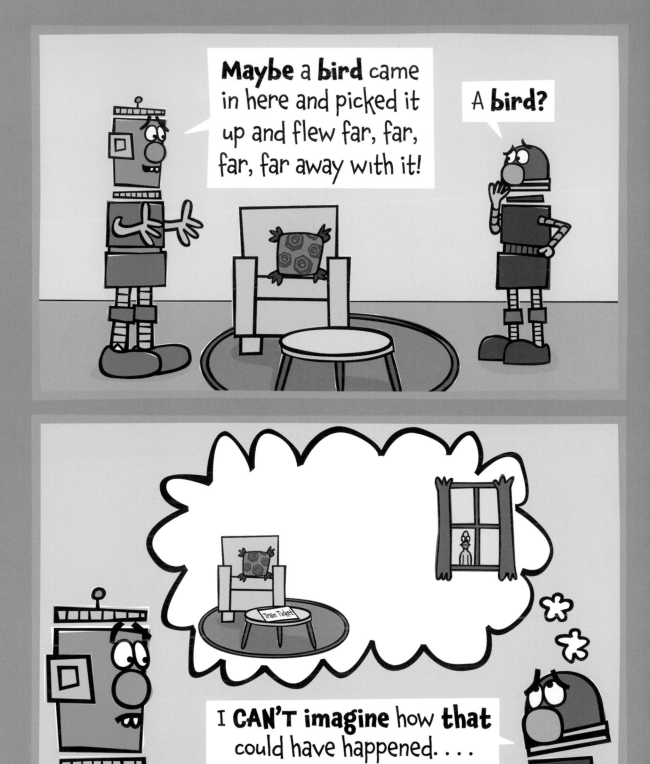

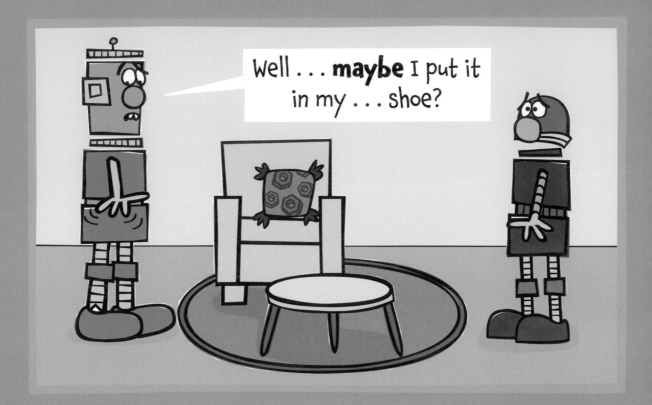

Well, I also **imagined** something. . . . I **imagined** what a train trip would be like **without you,** Blue Robot. . . .

I **imagined** it would be **sad . . . !**

I **imagined** it would be **lonely!**